Dirty Limericks

Anonymous

with an Introduction by
Brian Aldiss

ALMA CLASSICS

ALMA CLASSICS
an imprint of

ALMA BOOKS LTD
3 Castle Yard
Richmond
Surrey TW10 6TF
United Kingdom
www.almaclassics.com

Dirty Limericks first published by Alma Classics in 2007
This new paperback edition first published by Alma Classics in 2017
Introduction © Brian Aldiss, 2007

Printed in the UK by CPI Group (UK) Ltd, Croydon CR0 4YY

ISBN: 978-1-84749-709-3

The texts included in the present edition are reprinted with
permission or presumed to be in the public domain. Every effort
has been made to ascertain and acknowledge their copyright status,
but should there have been any unwitting oversight on our part, we
would be happy to rectify the error in subsequent printings.

Contents

Introduction

British ballads have come and more or less gone. The mark of these common songs and rhymes is that they address someone:

> You married men whom Fate has assigned
> To marry with them that are too much kind.

Or they may quote a higher authority:

> Says my uncle, I pray you discover
> What hath been the cause of your woes.

Or they may speak out for a group:

> Six jolly wee miners, an' miner lads are we.

Mostly these humble poems express dissatisfaction with one aspect or another of life. All rather similar to the blues which superseded them. In general, they are local complaints.

The limerick, that wily serpent, is written by a different kind of person. This person has no time for jolly wee miners and country lasses, unless they can be made to form the subject of a striking moral deficiency. The limerick writer is more sophisticated, and appears to be well travelled; he knows what is painted on a shutter in Calcutta, or what punishment the Bishop of Birmingham meted out, or the complications in the life of a prostitute in Rangoon, or the uses for clay in Bombay, and so on. He is a worldly person, generally a man, whose geographical knowledge extends throughout the British Empire. Indeed, the heyday of the limerick was very likely the heyday of the Empire, only a generation or two ago.

We imagine a sturdy District Commissioner, sitting on his veranda, *chota peg* by his side, summing up the misfortunes of a young girl from Madras in five succinct lines. No fool he. Immorality and perversions fail to shock him. Indeed, the more surreal they are, the better. They may take place in underground aviaries, in a rather dusty cave outside Belgrave, by a punt-fraught river near Buckingham, or in a crowd at Stroud.

Our connoisseur of the curious has to master an intricate rhyme scheme: AABBA. It is not a format for weaklings.

The first limerick I was told when a juvenile may have been composed by another juvenile. I quote it merely for antiquarian purposes:

There was a young lady from Riga
Who had an affair with a tiger.
The result of the fuck
Was a paralysed duck,
Two goats and a circumcised spider.

At the age of five, when I had been so recently the product of a gynaecological event myself, this even more unlikely outcome may have seemed amusing. But the folly of the putative bard went even deeper: the rhyme scheme does not work. "Spider" does not rhyme with either "tiger" or "Riga". The menagerie as described is impossible. Better perhaps to concentrate on the parturition which followed the affair:

Poor girl! Her long labour
Was described by a neighbour
Like Frankenstein climbing the Eiger.

While this is not particularly good, rhyme receives better consideration. The amateur rhymester did not foresee, before setting out, that the only word to rhyme with "tiger", apart from "Eiger" is "Geiger", usually linked with "counter". So he is stuck and, in a desperate attempt to amuse, comes up with a "circumcised spider" – not at all likely, practical or funny, even to spider lovers.

One more insuperable objection must be raised in connection with this limerick. At the mouth of the Western Dvina in Latvia stands an undistinguished city known as Riga. The city's name is pronounced *reega*, not *ryger*. I rest my case.

Better in every way to stick to the British Empire. Or at least to what was part of the British Empire, as in the following example, newly to hand:

There was a young man of Mumbai
Who ravished a sow in her sty.
He was deeply offended
To note, when he'd ended,
She'd been lying there just watching the sky.

Here are two more by my own pen:

There was a young chap from out yonder
Who buggered a big anaconda,
He regretted this crime
For the rest of his time,
While the reptile grew fonder and fonder.

Said a whore to the priest of Cahors,
"You're the worst lay in all Perigord.
You smell and you're drunk
And I'm covered in spunk
And – bon Dieu! – there's the Pope at the door!

As I have demonstrated, a good limerick has many difficulties to surmount. It is a surreal verse form which deserves better recognition, more approbation. This book should help it greatly on its way.

– Brian Aldiss, 2007

Editor's Note

It has been my aim to introduce the limerick phenomenon at its most playful to as many new readers as possible. To this end, I have collected those I consider the very finest "dirty limericks" for this edition. For those not entirely new to the tradition, some of the classics included will have been encountered before, perhaps at the bar, or around a dining table, or in previous anthologies. Hopefully there will be plenty of new items to grace aficionados' personal collections among the five categories of recurrent themes into which I've divided this distillation of a lifetime's exchange with fellow enthusiasts. Certainly the sixth and final category entitled "Original" ought to guarantee some novelty, with its revelation that Shakespeare's use of the occasional dirty limerick drew on a pre-established tradition from at least as far back as the fourteenth Century.

It is a frustrating characteristic of the more modern, largely twentieth-century dirty-limerick tradition that the authorship of these fine literary achievements has become more and more difficult to ascertain with the passing of time. Even where authorship is suspected, one often finds that the truth is ambiguous because the author – a bishop's wife perhaps, or a headmaster – preferred to remain anonymous. And sometimes a limerick has been told to me as though invented by the teller, only for me to find it was an adapted version of yet another fellow enthusiast's favourite from one of the previous uncredited collections to have appeared in print. Hence no credits appear in these pages. If any reader of this collection feels they have not received due acknowledgement, I hope they will accept both my apologies and my congratulations for their genius. They certainly deserve to be recognized for their role in perpetuating such an insightful strand of the Anglo-Saxon literary tradition. In humbled recognition of my own lack of ingenuity, I have chosen to publish this edition under the authorship of the collective Anonymous who are its true authors.

Dirty Limericks

Geographical

I

There was a young man from Kildare,
Who was having his girl on the stair;
On the forty-fourth stroke,
The banister broke
And he finished her off in mid-air.

II

There was a young girl of Baroda
Who built herself a pagoda.
The walls of its halls
Were hung with the balls
And the tools of the fools that bestrode her.

III

There was a young girl of Cape Cod
Who thought babies were fashioned by God.
But it was not the Almighty
Who lifted her nightie –
It was Roger the lodger, that sod!

IV

There was a young man of Cape Horn
Who wished he had never been born;
And he wouldn't have been
If his father had seen
That the end of the rubber was torn.

V

There was a young lady of Norway
Who hung by her toes in a doorway.
She said to her beau:
"Just look at me, Joe,
I think I've discovered one more way."

VI

There was a young fellow of Warwick
Who had reason for feeling euphoric,
For he could by election
Have triune erection:
Ionic, Corinthian, Doric.

VII

A crooner who lived in West Shore
Caught both of his balls in a door.
Now his mezzo-soprano
Is rather piano
Though he was a loud basso before.

VIII

There was a young girl from Sofia
Who succumbed to her lover's desire.
She said, "It's a sin,
But now that it's in,
Could you shove it a few inches higher!"

IX

There was a young lady of Louth
Who returned from a trip to the South.
Her father said, "Nelly,
There's more in your belly
Than ever went in by your mouth."

X

There was a young man from Devizes
Whose balls were of two different sizes.
One was so small
It was nothing at all
The other took numerous prizes.

XI

A baritone star of Havana
Slipped horribly on a banana;
He was sick for a year
Then resumed his career
As a promising lyric soprano.

XII

There was a young girl from Pitlochry
Who was had by a man in a rockery
She said, "Oh! You've cum
All over my bum;
This ain't good sex – it's a mockery!"

XIII

There was a young man from Axminster
Whose designs were quite base and quite sinister.
His lifelong ambition
Was anal coition
With the wife of the French foreign minister.

XIV

A young woman got married at Chester,
Her mother she kissed and she blessed her.
Said she, "You're in luck,
He's a stunning good fuck –
I've had him myself down in Leicester."

XV

There was a young man from Racine
Who invented a fucking machine:
Both concave and convex,
It would fit either sex,
With attachments for those in between.

XVI

A sprightly old roué from Buckingham
Used to walk by the river at Luckingham
And study the stunts
Of the cunts in the punts
And the tricks of the pricks that were fucking 'em.

XVII

There was a young man from Berlin
Whose tool was the size of a pin.
Said his girl with a laugh
As she fondled his shaft,
"Well, *this* won't be much of a sin."

XVIII

There was a young harlot from Kew
Who filled her vagina with glue.
She said with a grin,
"If they pay to get in,
They'll pay to get out of it, too."

XIX

There was a young man of Bengal
Who went to a fancy dress ball.
Just for a whim
He dressed as a quim
And was had by the dog in the hall.

XX

There was a young man from Natal
And Sue was the name of his gal.
He went out one day
For a rather long way –
In fact, right up Sue'z Canal.

XXI

There was a young lady of Dee
Went to bed with each man she would see.
When it came to a test
She wished to be best,
And practice makes perfect, you see.

XXII

Three lovely young girls from St Thomas
Attended dance halls in pyjamas.
They were fondled all summer
By sax, bass and drummer –
I'm surprised that by now they're not mamas.

XXIII

There was a young Turkish cadet,
And this is the damnedest one yet –
His prick was so long,
And so pointed and strong,
He could bugger six Greeks *en brochette*.

XXIV

There was a young girl of Asturias
With a penchant for practices curious.
She loved to bat rocks
With her gentlemen's cocks –
A practice both rude and injurious.

XXV

There was a young bloke of Havant
Whose conduct, I'd say, was gallant
For he slept with his dozens
Of nieces and cousins
And always had time for his aunt.

XXVI

There was an old girl from Kilkenny
Whose usual charge was a penny,
But for half of that sum
You could fondle her bum –
A source of amusement to many.

XXVII

Nymphomaniacal Alice
Used a dynamite stick for a phallus;
They found her vagina
In North Carolina
And half of her asshole in Dallas.

XXVIII

There was a young lady in Reno
Who lost all her dough playing keno.
But she lay on her back
And opened her crack –
And now she owns the casino.

XXIX

There was a young man from Belgrave
Who found a dead whore in a cave.
He said, "It's disgusting –
But she only needs dusting –
And think of the money I'll save!"

XXX

There was a young lady of Wantage
Of whom the Town Clerk took advantage.
Said the County Surveyor,
"Of course you must pay her;
You've altered the line of her frontage."

XXXI

There was a young lady of Brussels
Whose pride was her vaginal muscles;
She could easily plex them
And so interflex them
As to whistle love songs through her bustles.

XXXII

There was a young man of Pitlochry
Whose morals were simply a mockery,
For under the bed
He'd a woman, instead
Of the usual item of crockery.

XXXIII

A widow who lived in Rangoon
Hung a black-ribboned wreath on her womb,
"To remind me," she said,
"Of my husband who's dead,
And of what put him into his tomb."

XXXIV

There was a young man of Belgravia
Who cared neither for God nor his Saviour.
He walked down the Strand
With his prick in his hand
And was jailed for indecent behaviour.

Sexual

I

There was a sailor at sea
Who came home as drunk as could be.
He wound up the clock
With the end of his cock,
And buggered his wife with the key.

II

A young violinist from Rio
Was seducing a lady named Cleo.
As she took down her panties
She said, "No andantes;
I want this allegro con brio!"

III

In the Garden of Eden lay Adam
Complacently stroking his madam,
And loud was his mirth
For he knew that on earth
There were only two balls – and he had 'em.

IV

Said Einstein, "I have an equation
Which science might call Rabelaisian.
Let P be virginity
Approaching infinity,
And U be a constant persuasion.

"Now if P over U be inverted
And the square root of U be inserted
X times over P,
The result, QED,
Is a relative," Einstein asserted.

V

A bobby of Nottingham Junction,
Whose organ had long ceased to function,
Deceived his good wife
For the rest of her life
With the aid of his constable's truncheon.

VI

There was a young fellow called Tupper
Who invited a girl home for supper.
They sat down to dine
At a quarter to nine,
And by twenty past ten he was up her.

VII

There was a young lady named Flo
Whose lover was almighty slow,
So they tried it all night
Till he got it just right
For practice makes pregnant, you know.

VIII

A salvation lassie named Claire
Was having her first love affair.
As she climbed into bed
She reverently said,
"I wish to be opened with prayer."

IX

Rosalina, a pretty young lass
Had a truly magnificent ass:
Not rounded and pink,
As you possibly think –
It was grey, had long ears, and ate grass.

X

There was a young lady at sea
Who complained that it hurt her to pee.
Said the ship's mate,
"That accounts for the state
Of the cook and the captain and me."

XI

There was a young fellow named Mick
Who fancied himself rather slick.
He went to a ball
Dressed in nothing at all
But a big velvet bow round his prick.

XII

There was a young lady named Banker
Who slept while her ship lay at anchor.
She awoke in dismay
When she heard the mate say:
"Hi: Hoist up the top-sheet and spanker!"

XIII

On her bosom a beauteous young frail
Had illuminated the price of her tail;
And on her behind,
For the sake of the blind,
The same was embroidered in Braille.

XIV

A man with venereal fear
Had intercourse in his wife's ear.
She said "I don't mind,
Except that I find
When the telephone rings, I don't hear."

XV

There was a young fellow named Dice
Who remarked, "They say bigamy's nice,
But even two are a bore,
So I'd prefer three or four,
For the plural of spouse, it is spice!"

XVI

There once was a dentist named Stone
Who saw a girl patient alone.
In a fit of depravity
He filled the wrong cavity,
And my, how his practice has grown!

XVII

The tax-paying whores of the nation
Sent Congress a large delegation
To convince those old fools
Their professional tools
Were subject to depreciation.

XVIII

"For the tenth time, dull Daphnis," said Chloe,
"You have told me my bosom is snowy;
You have made much fine verse on
Each part of my person,
Now *do* something – it don't need to be showy!"

XIX

A nudist resort in Benares
Took a midget in all unawares.
Then he made members weep
For he just couldn't keep
His nose out of private affairs.

XX

There was a young plumber named Lee
Who was plumbing a young girl by the sea.
She said, "Stop your plumbing,
There's somebody coming!"
Said the plumber, still plumbing, "It's me."

XXI

The Shah of the Empire of Persia
Lay for days in a sexual merger.
When the nautch asked the Shah,
"Won't you ever withdraw?"
He replied, "It's not love; it's inertia."

XXII

A young trapeze artist named Bract
Is faced by a very sad fact.
Imagine his pain
When, again and again,
He catches his wife in the act!

XXIII

A fellow with passions quite gingery
Was exploring his young sister's lingerie;
Then with giggles of pleasure
He plundered her treasure –
Adding incest to insult and injury.

XXIV

There was a young man from the Coast
Who had an affair with a ghost.
At the height of orgasm,
This she-ectoplasm,
Said, "I think I can feel it – almost."

XXV

There was a young man called Astaire
Who was having a girl in a chair.
At the sixty-third stroke
The furniture broke
And his rifle went off in the air.

XXVI

An impetuous couple named Kelly
Now go through life belly-to-belly
Because in their haste
They used library paste
Instead of petroleum jelly.

XXVII

While Titian was mixing rose madder
His model posed nude on a ladder.
Her position, to Titian,
Suggested coition,
So he climbed up the ladder and 'ad 'er.

XXVIII

A wanton girl with wit she used nimbly,
Reproached for not acting more primly,
Answered, "Heaven's above!
I know sex isn't love,
But it's such an attractive facsimile."

XXIX

For the prick-naming prize of Pinole
This year's winner was Daniel O'Dole.
He will tell you with bonhomie.
"I call mine 'Metonymy',
Because it's a part of the whole."

XXX

There was a young student named Jones
Who'd reduce any maiden to moans
By his wonderful knowledge,
Acquired in college,
Of nineteen erogenous zones.

XXXI

There was a young fellow named Bliss
Whose sex life was strangely amiss,
For even with Venus
His recalcitrant penis
Would never do better than t
                              h
                                i
                              s.

XXXIII

If intercourse gives you thrombosis
While continence causes neurosis,
I prefer to expire
Fulfilling desire
Than live on in a state of psychosis.

XXXIV

A mathematician named Hall
Had a hexahedronical ball,
And the cube of its weight
Times his pecker, plus eight,
Was four fifths of five eighths of fuck-all.

XXXV

A colonel unashamed at being bent,
Who lived in a lavender tent,
Said that some sessions
With interesting Hessians
Had taught him what war really meant.

XXXVI

There was an aesthetic young Miss
Who thought it the apex of bliss
To jazz herself silly
With the bud of a lily,
Then go to the garden and piss.

XXXVII

There was a young girl from old Gloucester
Whose parents were sure they had lost her,
Till they came in the grass
To the marks of her ass
And the knees of the man who had crossed her.

XXXVIII

There was a young fellow of Kent
Whose prick was so long that it bent,
So to save himself trouble
He put it in double,
And instead of coming he went.

Bestial

I

There was a young peasant named Gorse
Who fell madly in love with his horse.
Said his wife, "You rapscallion,
That horse is a stallion –
This constitutes grounds for divorce."

II

There was an old Scot named McTavish
Who attempted an anthropoid ravish.
The object of rape
Was the wrong sex of ape,
And the anthropoid ravished McTavish.

III

There was a young gaucho named Bruno
Who said, "Screwing is one thing I *do* know.
A woman is fine,
And a sheep divine,
But a llama is Numero Uno."

IV

There was a young lady of Rhodes
Who sinned in unusual modes.
At the height of her fame
She abruptly became
The mother of four dozen toads.

V

There was a young girl of Dundee
Who was raped by an ape in a tree.
The result was most horrid –
All ass and no forehead,
Three balls and a purple goatee.

VI

There was a young man of Seattle
Who bested a bull in a battle.
With fire and with gumption
He assumed the bull's function,
And deflowered the whole herd of cattle.

VII

A vice both obscene and unsavoury
Holds the Mayor of Southampton in slavery.
With bloodcurdling howls
He deflowers young owls
Which he keeps in an underground aviary.

VIII

There was a young man from Peru
Who attempted to bugger a gnu.
Said the gnu, "Pederasty
Is decidedly nasty,
But you may slip up my slew for a sou."

IX

A disgusting young man named McGill
Made his neighbours exceedingly ill;
When they learned of his habits
Involving white rabbits
And a bird with a flexible bill.

X

There once was a fellow named Siegel
Who attempted to bugger a beagle,
But the mettlesome bitch
Turned and said with a twitch,
"It's fun, but you know it's illegal."

XI

A herder who hailed from Terre Haute,
Fell in love with a young nanny goat;
The daughter he sired
Was greatly admired
For her beautiful angora coat.

XII

There was a young lad of St John's
Who wanted to bugger the swans
But the loyal hall porter
Said "No! Take my daughter.
Them birds is reserved for the dons."

XIII

There was an old jockey named Rains
Possessed of more ballocks than brains.
He stood on a stool
To bugger a mule,
And got kicked in the balls for his pains.

XIV

There was a young person of Jaipur
Who fell madly in love with a viper.
With screams of delight
He'd retire every night
With the viper concealed in his diaper.

XV

A lady while dining at Crewe
Found an elephant's whang in her stew.
Said the waiter, "Don't shout,
Or wave it about,
Or the others will be wanting one too."

XVI

There was an old man of the Cape
Who buggered a Barbary ape.
Said the ape: "Sir your prick
Is too long and too thick,
And something is wrong with the shape."

XVII

There was a young fellow of Kent
Who had a peculiar bent:
He collected the turds
Of various birds
And had them for lunch during Lent.

XVIII

A farmer I know named O'Doole
Has a long and incredible tool.
He can use it to plough
Or to diddle a cow
Or just as a cue-stick at pool.

XIX

There was a young man of Peru
Who was hard up for something to do
So he took out his carrot
And buggered his parrot
And sent the results to the zoo.

XX

An old maid in the land of Aloha
Got wrapped in the coils of a Boa.
And as the snake squeezed
The old maid, not displeased,
Cried, "Darling! I love it! Sa'moa!"

Lavatorial

I

There was a young fellow named Chivy
Who, whenever he went to the privy,
First solaced his mind,
And then wiped his behind,
With some well-chosen pages of Livy.

II

I dined with the Duchess of Leigh
Who asked, "Do you fart when you pee?"
I said with some wit,
"Do you belch when you shit?"
And felt it was one-up for me.

III

"It's true," confessed Lady Jane Torres,
"That I often beg lifts in lorries.
When the men stop to piss
I see things that I miss
When I travel alone in my Morris."

IV

There was a young fellow named Bart
Who strained every shit through fart.
Each tip-tapered turd
Was the very last word
In this deft and intricate art.

V

There was a young man from Montmartre
Who was famed far and wide for his fart.
When they said, "What a noise!"
He replied with great poise,
"When I fart, sir, I fart from the heart."

VI

Q. Flaccus in his third liber:
"The Romans have no wood-pulp fibre.
A crapulent quorum
Will squat in the Forum
And heave dirty stones in the Tiber."

VII

There was a young Royal Marine
Who tried to fart 'God Save the Queen'.
When he reached the soprano
Out came the guano,
And his breeches weren't fit to be seen.

VIII

There was an old lady of Cyprus
Who got shot in the ass by some snipers,
And when she blew air
Through the holes that were there,
She astonished the Cameron Pipers.

IX

There was a young lady of Rheims,
Who amazingly pissed in four streams.
A friend poked around
And a coat button found
Wedged tightly in one of her seams.

X

There was a young friar of Byhill
Who went up to shit on a high hill.
When the abbot asked, "Was it
A goodly deposit?"
He said, *"Vox et praeterea nihil."*

XI

There was a young fellow from Leeds
Who swallowed a packet of seeds.
Great tufts of grass
Sprouted out of his ass
And his balls were all covered with weeds.

XII

There was a young man from Kilbride
Who fell in a shit house and died.
His heart-broken brother
Fell into another,
And now they're interred side by side.

XIII

I once knew a very queer lass
Who had a triangular ass.
Now it might sound absurd
But the shape of her turd
Was a stately pyramidal mass!

XIV

Sir Reginald Barrington, Bart.
Went to the masked ball as a fart.
He had painted his face
Like a more private place,
And his voice made the dowagers start.

XV

There was a young man of Madras
Whose balls were constructed of brass.
When jangled together
They played 'Stormy Weather'
And lightning shot out of his ass.

XVI

A flatulent nun of Beliah
One Easter eve supped on papaya,
Then honoured the Passover
By turning her ass over
And obliging with Handel's *Messiah*.

XVII

An impish young fellow named James
Had a passion for idiot games.
He lighted the hair
Of his lady's affair
And laughed as she peed through the flames.

XVIII

There was a young lady of Ealing,
Endowed with such delicate feeling,
When she read on the door:
"Don't piss on the floor" –
She lay down and pissed on the ceiling.

XIX

There was a young lady of Dexter
Whose husband exceedingly vexed her,
For whenever they'd start
He'd unfailingly fart
With a blast that damn nearly unsexed her.

XX

There was a young lady named Skinner
Who dreamt that her lover was in her.
She woke with a start
And let out a fart
That was followed by luncheon and dinner.

Clerical and Institutional

I

There were two young ladies of Birmingham,
And this is a scandal concerning 'em.
They lifted the frock
And tickled the cock
Of the Bishop engaged in confirming 'em.

Now the Bishop was nobody's fool,
For he'd been to a good public school,
So he took down their britches
And buggered those bitches
With his ten inch Episcopal tool.

But this didn't worry those two;
Said they, as the Bishop withdrew,
"The vicar is quicker
And thicker and slicker,
And longer and stronger than you."

II

There was an archbishop in France
Who saw a nude woman by chance.
The result, I affirm,
Was emission of sperm
In the archiepiscopal pants.

III

There once was a priest of Gibraltar
Who wrote dirty jokes in his Psalter.
An inhibited nun
Who read every one
Made a vow to be laid on his altar.

IV

There was a young monk from Siberia
Whose morals were very inferior.
He did to a nun
What he shouldn't have done,
And now she's a Mother Superior.

V

I once had the wife of a Dean
Seven times while the Dean was out skiin'.
She remarked with some gaiety,
"Not bad for the laity,
Though the Bishop once managed thirteen."

VI

There was a young lady named Alice
Who peed in a Catholic chalice.
The Padre agreed
It was done out of need,
And not out of Protestant malice.

VII

There was a young lady of Chichester
Who made all the saints in their niches stir.
One morning at matins
Her breasts in white satin
Made the Bishop of Chichester's britches stir.

VIII

There was a young student from Yale
Who was getting his first piece of tail.
He shoved in his pole,
But in the wrong hole,
And a voice from beneath yelled: "No sale!"

IX

"Well, madam," the Bishop declared,
While the Vicar just mumbled and stared,
"'Twere better, perhaps,
In the crypt or the apse,
Because sex in the nave must be shared."

X

The Bishop of Ibu Plantation
Wrote a thesis on Transfiguration
For the *Christian Review*
(As all good Bishops do)
While practising miscegenation.

XI

When the Bishop of Solomon's diocese
Was stricken with elephantiasis,
The public beheld
His balls as they swelled
By paying exorbitant priocese.

XII

From the depths of the crypt at St Giles
Came a scream that resounded for miles.
Said the vicar, "Good gracious!
Has Father Ignatius
Forgotten the Bishop has piles?"

XIII

An old archaeologist, Throstle,
Discovered a marvellous fossil.
He knew from its bend
And the knob on the end
'Twas the peter of Paul the Apostle.

XIV

A lecherous Bishop of Peoria,
In a state of constant euphoria,
Enjoyed having fun
With a whore or a nun
While chanting the Sanctus and Gloria.

XV

A licentious old justice of Salem
Used to catch all the harlots and jail 'em.
But instead of a fine
He would stand 'em in line,
With his common-law tool to impale 'em.

XVI

There once was a warden of Wadham
Who approved of the folkways of Sodom,
For a man might, he said,
Have a very poor head
But be a fine fellow, at bottom.

XVII

There was a young student of Oriel
Who flouted the ruling proctorial.
He ran down the corn
With a hell of a horn,
And buggered the Martyrs' Memorial.

XVIII

A young curate, quite new to the cloth,
At sex was surely no sloth.
He preached masturbation
To his whole congregation,
And was washed down the aisle on the froth.

XIX

There was a young monk of Kilkyre
Who was smitten with carnal desire.
The immediate cause
Was the abbess's drawers,
Which were hung up to dry by the fire.

XX

A lax Catholic layman called Fox
Makes his living by sucking off cocks.
In spells of depression
He goes to confession,
And jacks off the priest in a box.

Original

I

The lion is wonderliche strong
& ful of wiles and wo;
& wether he pleye
other take his preye
he can not do but slo (slay).

'Harleian MS 7322', *c*.14th century

II

From the hagg & hungry Goblin.
That into rags would rend yee,
& the spirit that stand's
by the naked man,
in the booke of moones defend yee…

Of thirty bare years have I
twice twenty bin enraged,
& of forty bin
three tymes fifteene
in durance soundlie cagèd

On the lordlie loftes of Bedlam
with stubble softe & dainty,
brave bracelets strong,
sweet whips ding dong
with wholesome hunger plenty…

'Tom o' Bedlam', trad. published 1615

III

For she had a tongue with a tang,
Would cry to a sailor, Goe hang!
She lov'd not the savour of Tar nor of Pitch
Yet a Tailor might scratch her where ere she did itch:
Then to Sea, Boyes, and let her goe hang!

William Shakespeare, *The Tempest*, Act ii, Sc. 2

IV

Tobacco's a Musician
And in a Pipe delighteth:
It descends in a Close
Through the Organ of the nose
With a Rellish that inviteth.

Barton Holyday, *Technogamia*, Act II, Sc. 3, 1618

V

Joane Easie got her a Nag and a Sledge
To the Privy-house for to slide, a:
The hole was beshit
That she could not sit,
But did cack as she lay on her side, a:

She was not wind
For she sent forth a sound
Did stretch her fundament wide, a.

'Joane Easie', pub. in *Wit and Drollery*, 1661

VI

My mither's ay glowran o'er me.
Tho she did the same before me:
I canna get leave
To look to my love,
Or else she'll be like to devour me…

'Katy's Answer to the young Laird',
pub. in *Tea Table Miscellany*, 1724

VII

There was an old woman of Leeds
Who spent all her life in good deeds;
She worked for the poor
Till her fingers were sore,
This pious old woman of Leeds.

John Harris, *The History of Sixteen Wonderful
Old Women*, pub. 1821

VIII

There was a sick man of Tobago,
Who liv'd long on rice-gruel and sago;
But at last, to his bliss,
The physician said this –
"To a roast leg of mutton you may go."

R.S. Sharpe, *Anecdotes and Adventures of Fifteen Gentlemen* (illustrated by R. Cruickshank), 1822

IX

There was an Old Man with a beard,
Who said, "It is just as I feared -
Two Owls and a Hen,
Four Larks and a Wren,
Have all built their nests in my beard!"

Edward Lear, *Book of Nonsense*, 1846